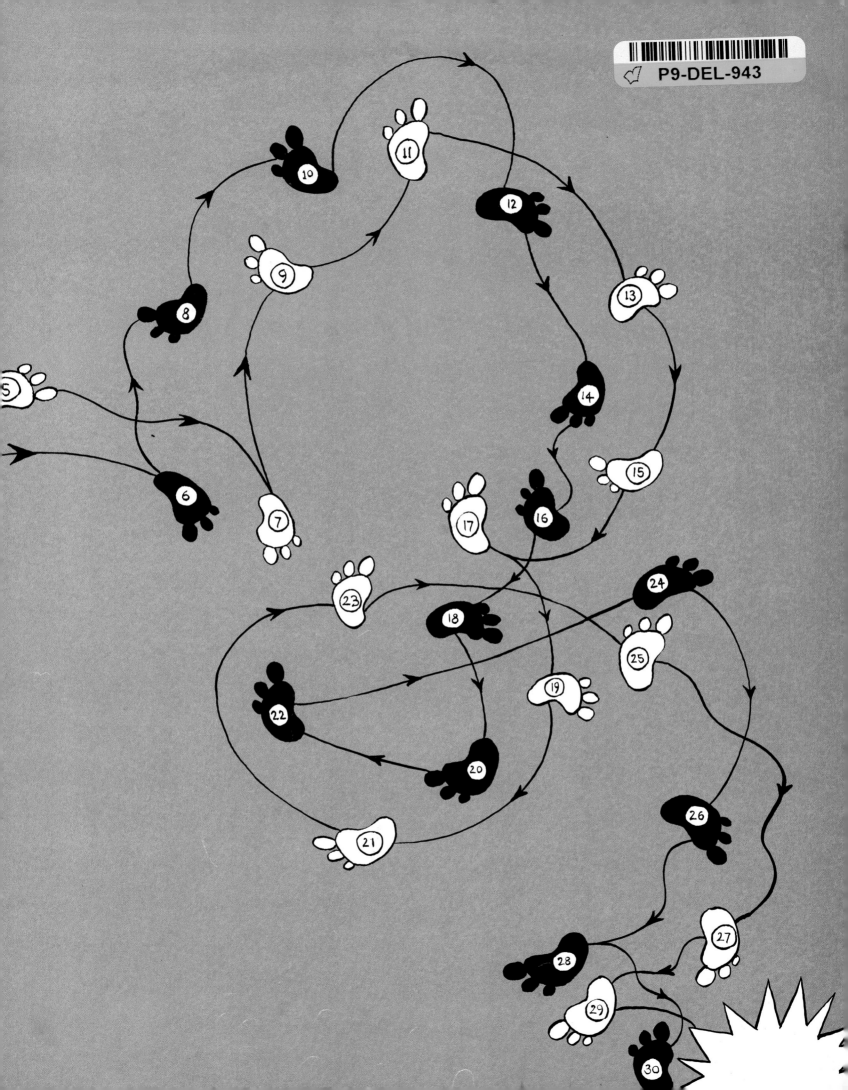

For Mary

Text and illustrations copyright © 2004 by Adam Stower

Published by Bloomsbury, New York and London
Distributed to the trade by Holtzbrinck Publishers

Library of Congress Cataloging-in-Publication Data
Stower, Adam.
Two left feet / Adam Stower.
p. cm.
Summary: Rufus, a monster who has trouble dancing due to his two left feet,
finds the perfect partner for the dance competition.
ISBN 1-58234-884-7 (alk. paper)
[1. Dance—Fiction. 2. Monsters—Fiction. 3. Contests—Fiction] I. Title.
PZ7.S89255 Tw 2004
[E] 22
2003047193

First U.S. Edition 2004
Printed in Hong Kong/China
1 3 5 7 9 10 8 6 4 2

Bloomsbury USA Children's Books
175 Fifth Avenue
New York, NY 10010

Two
Left Feet

Adam Stower

BLOOMSBURY
CHILDREN'S
BOOKS

Carved into the cliffs below the Glittering Palace is a dungeon world where the monsters live.

Every night the monsters are at the disco because, as everybody knows, monsters just love to dance.

Rufus and his friends are always there,
doing *their* own special dances.

Legs Twists,

Poppy Wiggles,

and Trevor Swings.

Tweet Flaps,

Sadie Shimmies,

and Flit Flutters.

And as for Rufus, he loves to dance
more than anybody.

But
Rufus is
a monster with two left
feet. Every time he tries
to dance, he just veers to
the right, going faster
and faster in smaller and
smaller circles,
until ...

WALLOP!
He falls flat on his little blue face. But his friends are always there to pick him up, dust him off, and tell him, "Well, you're certainly the best at the Wallop, so don't worry." And Rufus never did, as long as he had his friends to dance with.

One night something very exciting happened. A messenger from the Glittering Palace arrived and announced,

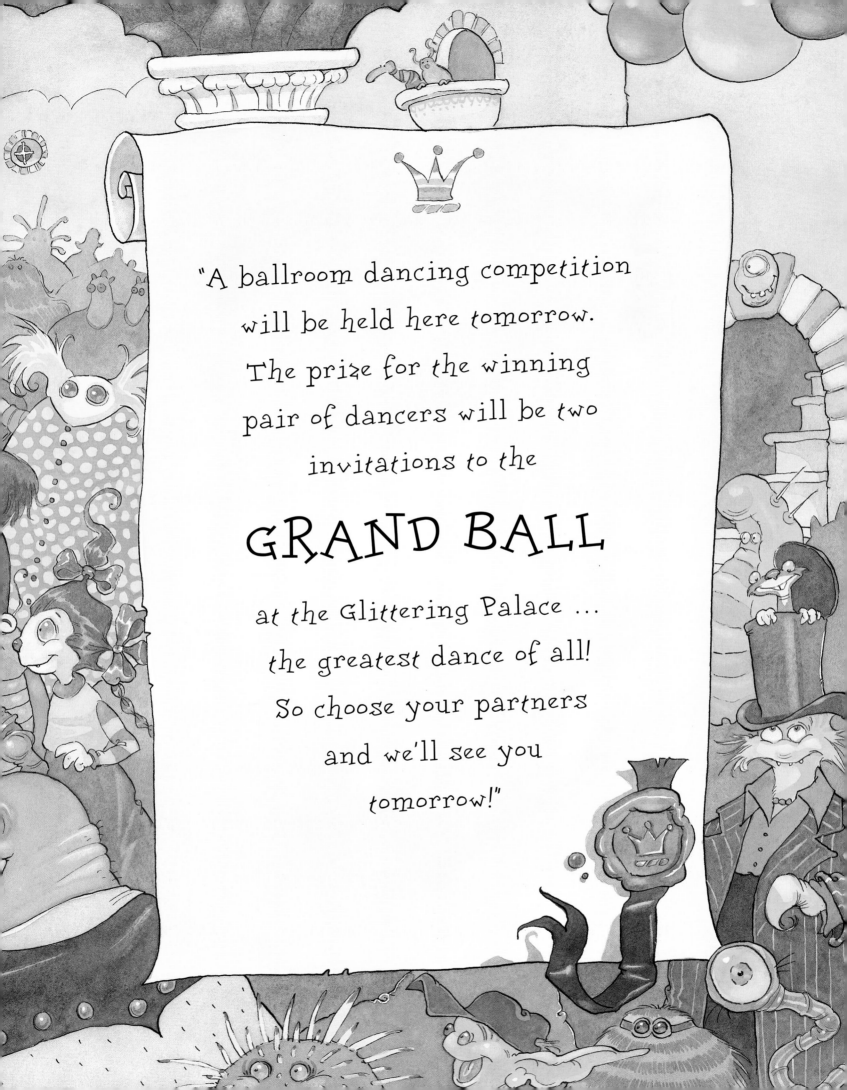

"A ballroom dancing competition will be held here tomorrow. The prize for the winning pair of dancers will be two invitations to the

GRAND BALL

at the Glittering Palace ... the greatest dance of all! So choose your partners and we'll see you tomorrow!"

Rufus immediately turned to his friends to find a partner for the competition. But everybody had already chosen somebody to dance with. Nobody had picked Rufus because he was the only one who couldn't dance without falling over. And in a flurry of excitement his friends headed for home, leaving Rufus feeling sad and lonely ...

... and all
because of his
two left feet!

Just then, Rufus heard a sniffle.

"Who's there?" he asked.
"Maddie," said a
little monster.
"Didn't you get
picked?" asked Rufus.
"No," said Maddie.
"I'm no good at dancing."
"Me neither," said Rufus.
"I can't Flutter, Swing, or Flap. I can't
Twist, Shimmy, or even Wiggle. All I can
do is the Wallop! But you and I
could go and watch
together, if you'd like?"
"I'd love to," said
Maddie.

So the following night, that's just what they did.
The band began to play, and the competition
was under way! Rufus cheered loudly for his
friends. They were each so good at their dances
that he was sure a pair of them would win.

However, it wasn't long before something odd started to happen.

Although his friends were very good at dancing by themselves, they had never danced in pairs before ...

First of all, Trevor's Swing went wild and knocked Tweet flat!
Then Legs Twisted one way when Poppy Wiggled the other, and
they were soon tied up in knots. And finally, Flit Fluttered into
Sadie's Shimmy and they crashed to the ground in a tangle of
eyes and tails!

The other monsters had similar trouble, and before long they were all piled in an enormous, giggling heap in the middle of the dance floor!

"Come on, Maddie!" laughed Rufus.
"We can't do any worse!" And with that,
they sprang up and began to dance.

That was when another odd thing happened.
Rufus and Maddie didn't go WALLOP!

Every time Rufus veered to his right, Maddie veered
to her left. To everyone's amazement, they were soon
spinning, skipping, and gliding from one corner
of the dance floor to the other in perfect harmony.

They were immediately declared *the* winners!
"I never *thought* we'd WIN!" laughed Rufus.
"Neither did I," said Maddie ...

"Not with two RIGHT feet!"

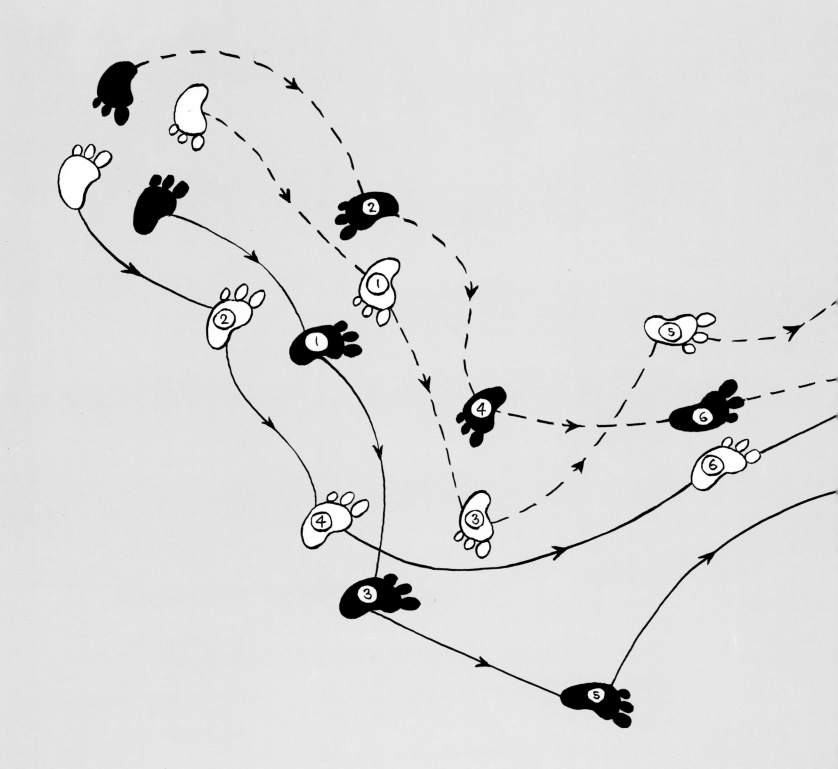